BONES
and the BIRTHDAY Mystery

A Viking Easy-to-Read

BY DAVID A. ADLER
ILLUSTRATED BY BARBARA JOHANSEN NEWMAN

VIKING

To Rachelli, Tzippora, Ayelet, Yakira, and Aharon. —D. A.

For Harry and Gloria. You guys rock. —B. J. N.

VIKING
Published by Penguin Group
Penguin Young Readers Group, 345 Hudson Street, New York, New York 10014, U.S.A.
Penguin Group (Canada), 90 Eglinton Avenue East, Suite 700, Toronto, Ontario, Canada M4P 2Y3
(a division of Pearson Penguin Canada Inc.)
Penguin Books Ltd, 80 Strand, London WC2R 0RL, England
Penguin Ireland, 25 St Stephen's Green, Dublin 2, Ireland (a division of Penguin Books Ltd)
Penguin Group (Australia), 250 Camberwell Road, Camberwell, Victoria 3124, Australia
(a division of Pearson Australia Group Pty Ltd)
Penguin Books India Pvt Ltd, 11 Community Centre,
Panchsheel Park, New Delhi – 110 017, India
Penguin Group (NZ), Cnr Airborne and Rosedale Roads, Albany, Auckland 1310,
New Zealand (a division of Pearson New Zealand Ltd)
Penguin Books (South Africa) (Pty) Ltd, 24 Sturdee Avenue, Rosebank,
Johannesburg 2196, South Africa

Penguin Books Ltd, Registered Offices: 80 Strand, London WC2R 0RL, England

First published in 2007 by Viking, a division of Penguin Young Readers Group

1 3 5 7 9 10 8 6 4 2

Text copyright © David A. Adler, 2007
Illustrations copyright © Barbara Johansen Newman, 2007
All rights reserved
Viking ® and Easy-to-Read ® are registered trademarks of Penguin Group (USA) Inc.

LIBRARY OF CONGRESS CATALOGING-IN-PUBLICATION DATA
Adler, David A.
Bones and the birthday mystery / by David A. Adler ; illustrated by Barbara Johansen Newman.
p. cm. — (Bones ; #5)
Summary: In his latest case, young Jeffrey Bones tries to discover
the whereabouts of his grandfather's missing birthday present.
ISBN-13: 978-0-670-06164-8 (hardcover)
ISBN-10: 0-670-06164-6
[1. Gifts—Fiction. 2. Birthdays—Fiction. 3. Grandfathers—Fiction. 4. Mystery and detective
stories.] I. Newman, Barbara Johansen, ill. II. Title. III. Series: Adler, David A. Bones ; #5.
PZ7.A2615Bob 2007
[E]—dc22
2006003511

Manufactured in China

-CONTENTS-

1. *Plop! Plop!*

"It's hot! It's hot!" Dad said.

He took a large cake from the oven.

He put it on the table.

It smelled so good!

"Don't taste it," Dad said.

"It's for Grandpa's party."

But it smelled so good!

Mom was making the icing.

"When the cake is cool," Mom said,

"you can ice it."

I waited.

I touched the cake.

It was still hot.

I waited and waited until it was cool.

"Hey, Mom. Hey, Dad.

May I take a tiny taste?

I'll cover it with icing.

No one will know."

Mom looked at Dad.

"Okay," Mom said,

"but just a tiny taste."

I took a tiny piece off the side.

Mmm!

The cake was good!

I took another tiny piece.

Mom gave me the bowl of icing.

I took a large spoon.

I filled it with icing

and held it over the cake.

Plop! Plop!

Icing fell onto the top of the cake.

I spread it around.

I turned the cake on its side.

I held up another spoonful of icing.

Plop! Plop!

Icing fell onto the side of the cake.

I spread it around.

I did that lots of times

until the cake was covered.

The table, my chair, my shirt, and my hands

were covered with icing, too.

I wondered if Grandpa would know

that I tasted his cake.

I took out my glass.

I looked at the cake.

The missing piece was covered.

"Hey," I said.

"The missing piece is missing!"

I always know when something is missing.

I'm a detective.

My name is Bones,

Detective Jeffrey Bones.

I find clues.

I solve mysteries.

2. I'm Not Uncle Fester

"Let's go," Dad said.

He took the cake.

Mom gave me the birthday card.

"It's Grandpa's gift," she said.

"A card is not a good gift," I said.

Mom said, "It's more than a card."

I knew what to do.

I'm a detective.

I held it up to the light

and looked through the envelope.

I only saw a card.

"Let's go," Dad said again.

I took my detective bag.

I always take it.

A good detective

must always be ready

to solve a mystery.

I sat in the back of the car.

Dad put the cake next to me.

Mom drove awhile.

Then she stopped.

"Hey," I said.

"Grandpa doesn't live here."

"It's Sally's house," Mom said.

"We're taking her to Grandpa's party."

Sally is Grandpa's friend.

She's nice.

Dad put the cake on my lap.

There was icing on the seat.

Dad wiped it off.

Sally sat in the back, next to me.

She had a big box on her lap.

It was wrapped and had a ribbon.

It was a gift for Grandpa.

When we got to Grandpa's house,

Dad took the cake.

Mom was about to ring the bell.

"Wait!" I said.

I took a fake beard, old hat,

and funny eyeglasses

from my detective bag

and put them on.

I rang the bell.

Grandpa opened the door.

He said, "Hello,"

to Mom, Dad, and Sally.

He looked at me and asked,

"And who are you?"

"Guess," I said.

"Uncle Fester?"

"No."

"Cousin Meko?"

"No."

I took off the beard,

hat, and eyeglasses.

"It's me," I said.

We hugged.

Then we went inside.

17

Lots of Grandpa's friends were there.

Dad gave Grandpa the cake

and said, "This is for you."

Sally gave Grandpa the box.

Mom said, "Jeffrey has a gift to give you.

It's a great gift. Hey," Mom asked me,

"where's Grandpa's birthday card?

Where's Grandpa's gift?"

3. It's a Surprise!

"Was it in a big box?" Fred asked.

Fred is Grandpa's friend.

"No," Mom said.

"It was in an envelope

with a birthday card."

"What fits in an envelope?" Jane asked.

She's Grandpa's friend, too.

"A small green picture of President Lincoln would fit," Fred said.

"The gift isn't money," Mom said.

Fred said, "Maybe it's a Willie Mays baseball card. I saw him play."

"No," Dad said.

"It's not a baseball card."

"Then what is it?" Sally asked.

"It's a surprise," Mom said.

"Well, I'll find it," I said.

"I'm a detective

and detectives find things."

I reached into my detective bag.

I took out my detective pen and pad.

I asked Mom when she last saw

Grandpa's birthday card.

"I gave it to you," Mom said.

She was right.

I wrote my name—*Jeffrey Bones*—

on my detective pad.

"Maybe it's in the car," I said.

We all went to the car.

The card wasn't there.

I even looked with my glass

and didn't find it.

"Maybe Jeffrey left it at home," Dad said.

"Let's go there and look," Mom said.

I told everyone,

"I'll find Grandpa's gift."

"I know you will," Grandpa said.

Before Mom, Dad, and I left,

I whispered to Grandpa,

"Please, save some cake for me."

Grandpa said he would.

4. I Solved the Mystery!

The kitchen was a mess.

Icing was everywhere.

We looked in the dish closet

and under the table

for Grandpa's birthday card.

I took out my detective pen and pad.

Table, I wrote on my pad.

23

I touched the icing on the table.

Sticky icing, I wrote on my pad.

I tasted the icing. *Yummy*, I wrote.

I put my pad down

and ate more icing.

"It's not here," Mom said.

"Let's go."

My hand stuck

to the detective pad.

The detective pad stuck to the table.

Dad said to me,

"It's too bad

we lost Grandpa's gift.

It was really a gift

for you and Sally, too."

A gift for me!

I thought about the birthday card.

Mom gave it to me

when I was in

the house.

In the car, I looked at the clues.

Jeffrey Bones, *Table*,

Sticky icing, and *Yummy*.

I looked at my detective pad.

It was stuck to me again.

"Sticky icing! That's it!"

I told Mom and Dad.

"I know where to find Grandpa's card.

I solved the mystery."

5. You'll See

"Where is it?" Mom and Dad asked.

"It's at Grandpa's," I said.

"But we looked," Mom said.

"We looked everywhere."

"No we didn't," I said.

I thought about the gift.

Dad said it was

for me and Sally, too.

"What's Grandpa's gift?" I asked.

"Is it really for me, too?"

"You'll see," Dad said.

When we got to Grandpa's house,

Grandpa, Sally, Fred, and Jane asked,

"Did you find the card?

Did you find the gift?"

The cake was still on the table.

Grandpa hadn't cut it.

He had waited for me.

"Your card was never lost," I said.

"Dad already gave it to you."

"He did?" Grandpa asked.

"I did?" Dad asked.

"I iced the cake," I said.

Mom said, "You iced your shirt

and pants, too."

"There was icing everywhere," I said.

"Even on the bottom of the cake plate.

"Grandpa's card was on my lap.

Dad put the cake on my lap.

The card stuck

to the bottom of the plate."

Grandpa looked under the cake plate

and there it was.

I had solved the mystery.

Grandpa opened the envelope

and read the card.

Then he showed us all

Mom and Dad's gift—

three tickets to the circus.

One ticket was for Grandpa.

One was for Sally,

and one was for me.

"I love the circus," I said.

Grandpa and Sally said

they love the circus, too.

We sang to Grandpa.

Then he cut the cake.

Even before he gave me a piece,

I knew I would love that, too.